A Note to Parents and Teachers

Kids can imagine, kids can laugh and kids can learn to read with this exciting new series of first readers. Each book in the Kids Can Read series has been especially written, illustrated and designed for beginning readers. Humorous, easy-to-read stories, appealing characters and topics, and engaging illustrations make for books that kids will want to read over and over again.

To make selecting a book easy for kids, parents and teachers, the Kids Can Read series offers three levels based on different reading abilities:

Level 1: Kids Can Start to Read

Short stories, simple sentences, easy vocabulary, lots of repetition and visual clues for kids just beginning to read.

Level 2: Kids Can Read with Help

Longer stories, varied sentences, increased vocabulary, some repetition and visual clues for kids who have some reading skills, but may need a little help.

Level 3: Kids Can Read Alone

More challenging topics, more complex sentences, advanced vocabulary, language play, minimal repetition and visual clues for kids who are reading by themselves.

With the Kids Can Read series, kids can enter a new and exciting world of reading!

Pup and Hound Play Copycats

For Allison and Emma, the copycat kids, and always, for Holly — S.H.

For Yvette, a copy cat ... and whisker accountant extraordinaire! — L.H.

⭐ Kids Can Read ® Kids Can Read is a registered trademark of Kids Can Press Ltd.

Text © 2007 Susan Hood
Illustrations © 2007 Linda Hendry

Kids Can Press acknowledges the financial support of the Government of Ontario, through the Ontario Media Development Corporation's Ontario Book Initiative; the Ontario Arts Council; the Canada Council for the Arts; and the Government of Canada, through the BPIDP, for our publishing activity.

Published in Canada by
Kids Can Press Ltd.
29 Birch Avenue
Toronto, ON M4V 1E2

Published in the U.S. by
Kids Can Press Ltd.
2250 Military Road
Tonawanda, NY 14150

www.kidscanpress.com

The artwork in this book was rendered in pencil crayon on a sienna colored pastel paper.
The text is set in Bookman.

Series editor: Tara Walker
Edited by Yvette Ghione
Printed and bound in Singapore

The hardcover edition of this book is smyth sewn casebound.
The paperback edition of this book is limp sewn with a drawn-on cover.

CM 07 0 9 8 7 6 5 4 3 2 1
CM PA 07 0 9 8 7 6 5 4 3 2 1

Library and Archives Canada Cataloguing in Publication

Hood, Susan
        Pup and hound play copycats / written by Susan Hood; illustrated by Linda Hendry.

(Kids Can read)
ISBN 978-1-55453-144-8 (bound)
ISBN 978-1-55453-145-5 (pbk.)

1. Dogs—Juvenile fiction. I. Hendry, Linda II. Title.
III. Series: Kids Can read (Toronto, Ont.)

PZ7.H758Puppl 2007   j813'.54   C2007-901119-5

Kids Can Press is a ,©rus™ Entertainment company

Pup and Hound
Play Copycats

Written by Susan Hood

Illustrated by Linda Hendry

Kids Can Press

What was that?

An old leather shoe!

Pup pulled it away.

He wanted it, too.

So Hound chased the ducks
quacking their song.

Pup dropped the shoe,

then tagged along.

Hound stopped to visit

the pigs eating slops.

Pup pushed in, too,

smacking his chops.

Hound needed a nap —

a short getaway.

But that tagalong pup

wanted to play.

Hound hid by a tree.

Pup did, too.

Hound hid in a bush.

Pup did, too.

Hound went through the gate.

"Woof!"

Pup did the same.

Poor Hound was tired

of playing this game.

Hound ran to the corn maze

as fast as he could.

If that didn't work,

then nothing would!

Ah! Alone at last.

"Arf!" Not so fast!

Humph! Hound stomped

off to a stream.

He crossed the log —

a high balance beam.

Of course, that pup followed.

Go back, silly dog!

Pup's legs were wobbly,

and so was the log.

Whoopsy! Pup slipped!

He fell — *ker-PLUNK!*

Hound woofed when he saw

poor Pup get dunked.

Hound leaped in

and pulled Pup out.

He licked poor Pup

on his soft, wet snout.

Pup licked his wet fur.

And Hound did, too.

Then Pup smelled dinner.

And Hound did, too.

Pup trotted home.

Time for some chow.

Guess who followed?

Hound's the copycat now!